My Unicorn Adventure With Mom

Written by Joany Kane   Paintings by Glorinda Marie

My Unicorn Adventure with Mom
© 2021
Joany Kane & Glorinda Marie

"**Unicorns are real!**" Mom proclaimed, her smile beaming bright. Her joy in that statement lit up my room, even though it was night.

I didn't want to doubt my mom, but I didn't believe her statement to be true. **Unicorns** can't possibly be real, they're magical critters... not like **a kangaroo!**

Mom tucked me in and wished that my dreams would be sweet. Tomorrow she promised, I'd be in for a treat. "A treat?!" I asked wanting a hint. "We're going to find a **unicorn**, she shared, with a joyful glint.

Our Unicorn adventure started in our backyard of **flowers**. Mom told me that her garden had very special powers. The dahlias and daisies welcomed bees, birds and butterflies. If we quietly waited, they would bring us a surprise.

A butterfly arrived, with glittering sparkle on his wing. As it fluttered among the flowers I could hear the bird sing. Mom explained that magic was coming, harkened by the bird song. Finding the home of the **unicorn** would not take us long.

I watched with wonder as a door
appeared in the trunk in our tree.
Mom took my hand and said,
"It's time for our **unicorn** adventure,
come with me."

We followed the butterfly through the
tree trunk door, stepping into a
Fairy Tale World filled with wonders
galore. We started down the path made
of **four leaf clovers** covered in dew...

When we came to a field where a bunch
of dandelions grew! We blew on the
dandelions, watching the
white tassels float in the air...

When a leprechaun leapt from the **clovers** giving us a scare! Our wishes would come true he told us as he danced an Irish jig. But we couldn't see the **unicorns** without a **mistletoe** sprig.

The **leprechaun** gave us the sprig and bid us a happy farewell. We started down the path when we met a **witch** conjuring a spell. "To see the **unicorns** my flying spell you will need, have a drink from my cauldron so you can pick up speed."

We drank from the cauldron
And then we took flight.
Looking down at the **Fairy Tale World**,
Oh what a sight!

We grabbed hold of a **rainbow** and slid
down it like a slide.
And landed on a giant lady bug
who offered us a ride.

We rode through a forest of pansies
purple and yellow.
A wise owl on a branch gave us a
hoot hoot and a hello.

We arrived at a castle, a cobblestone building so grand. A handsome young knight greeted us by extending his hand. "Welcome to my castle, my name is Vince. This **magical** world is my kingdom, I am its prince."

We gave him the mistletoe sprig
and he kissed our hands.
He told us his kingdom had the most
unicorns in all of the **Fairy Tale** lands.

The prince took us to the vale where we looked on in awe. A valley filled with a dozen pink unicorns is what we saw!

"**Unicorns** ARE real," I exclaimed as my
mom gave me a warm smile.
So did the prince, (a memory I'd hold dear
for much longer than awhile.)

We watched as the **unicorns** danced and played. Together we all frolicked in that enchanted glade.

We snacked on snickerdoodles and drank mint ale. At the end of our wonderous day, in the prince's sleigh we set sail.

He took us back to the magical door in the tree. We said goodbye to the prince, my mom and me.

We were back in our yard safely at home, and discovered the prince had given us a gnome. The gnome was to guard and to guide. He'd bring us back to the prince, and down that **rainbow** we'd slide.

That night I was so tired I couldn't wait to fall asleep. After such an adventure with mom I knew my dreams would be sweet. We met a prince, found **unicorns** and a magical world filled with treasure...

But the **best part** was being with mom who I love beyond measure.

This is dedicated to Joany's mom Esther
Glorinda's mom Dolores
Glorindas's daughter Angelina (who is a mom)
To our friend Terri Potts & her mom Dee
To all moms (and daughters) xo xo xo

Glorinda & Joany met making a Christmas movie!

Joany wrote the screenplay, "The Christmas Card" & the movie premiered on the Hallmark Channel in 2006. Glorinda co-starred in the film.

The movie broke all-time ratings records & received an Emmy nomination. To this day it is a treasured fan favorite. Glorinda & Joany have been dear friends ever since.

Joany wrote this story to honor her beloved mom who loved unicorns. When Joany saw Glorinda had posted some of her art on Facebook she reached out to her believing Glorinda's whimsical, magical and joyful artists eye would be a perfect fit for the story.

A **unicorn** adventure partnership was formed! Stay tuned for more adventures!

Since Christmas brought Joany and Glorinda together, they put in some Christmas treasures into the story and paintings.

The story mentions the mistletoe sprig and a sleigh.

Can you find the other Christmas treasures in the paintings?

Star & Trees

Wreath

Poinsettia

Stocking filled with treats for you!

Presents filled with love!

It's a Candy Cane horn!

The gnome also subs as a Santa Elf! ☺

Reindeer pulling sleigh with jingle bells & bows

Thank you for going on this adventure with us!

When Joany & Glorinda were working on this book together, Glorinda would sign her emails & messages in the most delightfully whimsical way...

With joy, butterfly kisses, pansy hugs and **unicorn** dreams!

SWEET
DREAMS!

May all
your
dreams
come
true!

Made in the USA
Las Vegas, NV
20 June 2021